Dear Parent:
Your child's love of readi...

Every child learns to read in a differe... speed. Some go back and forth between ... favorite books again and again. Others read throu... order. You can help your young reader improve and beco... ...e confident by encouraging his or her own interests and abilities. From books your child reads with you to the first books he or she reads alone, there are I Can Read Books for every stage of reading:

SHARED READING
Basic language, word repetition, and whimsical illustrations, ideal for sharing with your emergent reader

BEGINNING READING
Short sentences, familiar words, and simple concepts for children eager to read on their own

READING WITH HELP
Engaging stories, longer sentences, and language play for developing readers

READING ALONE
Complex plots, challenging vocabulary, and high-interest topics for the independent reader

ADVANCED READING
Short paragraphs, chapters, and exciting themes for the perfect bridge to chapter books

I Can Read Books have introduced children to the joy of reading since 1957. Featuring award-winning authors and illustrators and a fabulous cast of beloved characters, I Can Read Books set the standard for beginning readers.

A lifetime of discovery begins with the magical words "I Can Read!"

Visit www.icanread.com for information
on enriching your child's reading experience.

Library of Congress catalog card number: 2013950468
ISBN 978-0-06-228498-3

Book design by Victor Joseph Ochoa

14 15 16 17 18   LP/WOR   10 9 8 7 6 5 4 3   ❖   First Edition

Rio 2

ONE Big BLUE FAMILY

by Catherine Hapka

HARPER

An Imprint of HarperCollinsPublishers

Blu was a blue Spix's Macaw.

That is one of the rarest

breeds of bird in the world.

In fact, before he moved to Rio,

Blu thought he was

the only one of his kind.

Then Blu met Jewel.

She was a blue Spix's Macaw

just like him!

Soon they were married.

"You're my one and only, Blu,"

Jewel said.

"Good thing," Blu joked,

"since I'm the only other one!"

Before long Blu and Jewel
had a family of their own.

Their three kids were named
Carla, Bia, and Tiago.
They had lots of fun
living in exciting Rio!

Blu and his family lived with
their human friends
Linda and Tulio.

One day, the humans made
a very important discovery.
They found a blue feather
deep in the Amazon jungle!

Could there be more blue macaws

like Blu out there somewhere?

Jewel wanted to find out.

So Blu packed his fanny pack.

Then they set off for the Amazon

with their family and friends.

Rafael, Pedro, and Nico
decided to go with
Blu's family.

They wanted to find some

new talent to audition

for their Carnaval show.

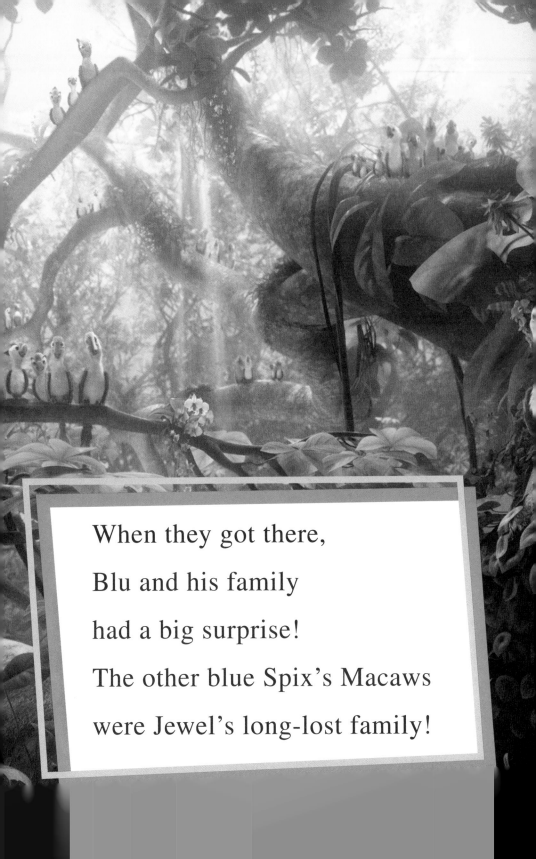

When they got there,
Blu and his family
had a big surprise!
The other blue Spix's Macaws
were Jewel's long-lost family!

Eduardo was the leader
of the flock.

He was Jewel's father.

He was gruff and tough
but lovable.
He thought his new son-in-law
was a little strange.

Blu also met Jewel's aunt Mimi.
Aunt Mimi thought Blu
was a little strange, too.
But she liked him anyway.

Then there was Roberto.

He was handsome and strong.

He had known Jewel

since they were tiny chicks.

Jewel was happy.

She was with her family again!

And she and Roberto

were still great friends.

But Blu didn't fit in very well
with these wild birds.
"What am I doing here?"
he asked his friends.

Eduardo tried to help Blu adjust.

He took Blu on a tour

through the jungle.

But Blu's survival skills
weren't up to the task.
"I just want to go back to Rio
and our normal lives!" he said.

Rafael, Nico, and Pedro
were Blu's best friends.
They wanted him to feel better,
so they gave him a pep talk.
"Go native!" Nico urged.
"Get wild!" Pedro added.

Blu decided his friends were right.

Jewel had come from the jungle.

The wild birds were her family.

That meant they couldn't be *all* bad.

Blu decided to do whatever it took

to fit in with Jewel's flock . . .

. . . and before long they were all
one happy big blue family!